Thomas the Tank Engine's

BIG BLUE TREASURY

BY CHRISTOPHER AWDRY
ILLUSTRATIONS BY KEN STOTT

Random House 🏠 New York

Thomas

AND THE TIGER

One day Thomas heard some children talking about a new wildlife park that was opening soon. "It's going to have lions and tigers and even a hippo," one boy said.

"What's a hippo?" Thomas asked.
"You'll see," said his driver. "We'll be carrying some of the animals to the park ourselves."

Soon the animals began to arrive. Some came by truck and some by rail. The engines worked very hard, pulling extra trains to carry them.

One morning Thomas' driver was particularly excited. "We're going to the harbor today to collect something special for the wildlife park," he told Thomas.

At the harbor they found a big crate containing a tiger
and her cubs. The tigers had come from a zoo far away.
A crane lifted the crate onto the train, and Thomas set off.

At the station Thomas waited while the big crate was unloaded. He was sad to see the tigers go.

He had been proud to carry such noble and
beautiful animals.
"I wonder if I shall see them again," he thought.

Near the station there was an old engine shed.
The workers used it for storing things they
did not use very often.

Later, when Thomas was passing the shed, he thought he saw something moving inside it. It seemed to look stripy.

Later that day Percy also passed the old engine shed.
He thought he saw some eyes glinting in the dark.

"I can't understand it," he told Thomas. "It was as if someone or something was watching me."

The next day Thomas was at the station.
He was listening to his driver talking to the fireman.

"It says in the newspaper that some tigers have escaped from the wildlife park," said the driver. "I wonder where they are?" Thomas smiled. He knew.

"Look in the old engine shed as we pass," he told his driver. When they came close, Thomas slowed down.

His driver looked out of the cab. "Why, it's the tiger and her cubs!" he said. "That was very smart of you to find them, Thomas."

Thomas' driver immediately told Sir Topham Hatt about the tigers.

"We'd better let their keeper know they're safe," said Sir Topham Hatt.

A truck came from the wildlife park to collect the tiger and her cubs. The keeper was very pleased.

"Well done, Thomas, for finding our tigers," he said.
Sir Topham Hatt agreed.
"You've been a Really Useful Engine," he said.

Thomas often sees the tiger and her cubs when he passes the park now. He feels very proud to have rescued them.

As a special thank-you, the keeper named one of the tiger cubs "Thomas."

Thomas

AND THE BIRTHDAY PARTY

"It's your driver's birthday on Saturday," said Percy.
"What is a birthday?" asked Thomas.
"It is the day when you get a year older," said Toby.

Thomas asked the fireman about the driver's birthday.
"His wife has baked him a cake," the fireman said.
"I wish I could see it," said Thomas.

"Let's give the driver a party at the station," said Toby.
"Then we can all see the cake!" said Percy.
The fireman went to ask the stationmaster.

The stationmaster agreed. The engines were very happy, but just two days before the birthday party Sir Topham Hatt sent Thomas away.

Thomas was sent to the big station to help out in the yard.
He was very upset.

At the big station Thomas worked hard all day.
He was looking forward to going home that evening.

But Sir Topham Hatt did not send Thomas home.
He was needed to work in the yard again the next day.

Thomas had to spend the night in the engine shed at the big station.

He could not get to sleep that night. "My driver will miss his party," he thought sadly.

The next day Sir Topham Hatt came. "Well done, Thomas," he said. "You have been working very hard. I am pleased with you."

"Thank you, sir," said Thomas. "But when can I go home?"
"Don't worry, Thomas. I know all about your secret,"
said Sir Topham Hatt. "We will get you home in time."

Saturday came and everyone began to get ready for the party. The stationmaster put up a sign saying HAPPY BIRTHDAY.

The porters decorated the engine shed and their children blew up the balloons. At five o'clock everything was ready.

But when Thomas came home that evening, there was
no sign of a party.

The shed doors were closed and it was silent everywhere.
"What has happened?" Thomas asked.

The driver was just getting down from the cab when
he saw his wife at the shed door.

She was carrying a big box. She took it into the shed, where everybody was waiting to greet the driver and shout "Happy birthday!"

The driver's wife took the lid off the box.
Thomas whistled loudly!
"The cake looks just like me," he said.

Everyone sang "Happy Birthday" around the cake.
"It looks too good to cut," said the driver,
but he cut it anyway.

The children climbed into one of the coaches for the party.

The driver said it was the nicest birthday he had ever had.

Thomas was happy, too.

James

AND THE BALLOONS

There was to be a balloon race on the Island of Sodor.
All the engines were very excited.

"I love balloons," said Thomas, "especially at parties when they go pop."
Gordon chuckled.

"But these are not party balloons," said Gordon.
"They are hot-air balloons with baskets fixed to them.
They carry people up into the sky."

James was chosen to take the balloons to their starting point. He was very proud.

"I wish I could watch the balloon race," he said.
"So do I," said his driver. "But we can't stop.
We have work to do."

Later that afternoon, as James puffed down the line,
he saw the balloons gently rising into the air.

"Can't we stop and watch for a while?" James sighed.
"I'm sorry, James," said his driver. "We're already late.
We must move on."

The balloons were high in the sky now. They drifted
overhead, but one sank very low.

"It looks as if that balloon is in trouble," said James.
His driver slowed down.

The balloon was almost down now. It bumped along
the ground and landed on the line right in front of James.
His driver put on the brakes.

"Thank you for stopping in time!" shouted one of the balloonists. "It looks as if we are out of the race."

"Never mind," replied James' driver. "We'll take you and your balloon to the finish."

James' driver and fireman helped the balloonists to pack their gear away.

Then they all heaved the heavy bundle onto the train.

The balloonists climbed aboard and James
started off again.

James reached the finish just in time to see the other balloons landing.

Lots of children were there to cheer the winner.

Thomas and Sir Topham Hatt were there, too.

"This is much more exciting than party balloons,"
said Thomas. Sir Topham Hatt agreed.

"And even more exciting if you rescue a balloon and bring it home!" said James.

Sir Topham Hatt laughed. "Well done, James," he said.